MEGA★MOUSE

MEGA BEAR

MOSQUITO MAN

MEGA PIG

MEGA CROC

MEGA PANDA

MEGA HIPPO

BUZZ! BUZZ!

A Firefly Book

Published by Firefly Books Ltd. 2015

Illustrations copyright © 2014 Mango Jeunesse, Paris
English translation copyright © 2015 Firefly Books

First printing

Publisher Cataloging-in-Publication Data (U.S.)

A CIP record for this title is available from the Library of Congress

Library and Archives Canada Cataloguing in Publication

A CIP record for this title is available from Library and Archives Canada

Published in the United States by
Firefly Books (U.S.) Inc.
P.O. Box 1338, Ellicott Station
Buffalo, New York 14205

Published in Canada by
Firefly Books Ltd.
50 Staples Avenue, Unit 1
Richmond Hill, Ontario L4B 0A7

Printed in China

MEGA·MOUSE

SÉVERINE VIDAL

BARROUX

How Mega Mouse
saved the kids on the bus

FIREFLY BOOKS

Mega Mouse is small, very small.
So to see her well,

you have to move closer.

Even closer.

She is such a sweet mouse, as you can see!

adorable ear

mischievous eye

charming smile

Mega Mouse treats hurt animals and helps children cross the street.

Mega Mouse is also the strongest of the Mega Animals. She is **unbeatable**.

She has a super disintegrating gun.

She isn't scared of anyone, not even the cruel **Mosquito Man**, the Big Wicked Mosquito thirsty for blood.

At her house, on Cheddar Street, she receives
the S.O.S. calls of the citizens of MegaCityVille.

They call her, she comes, she saves the day
and then drinks a cup of tea with her friends.

In short, let's say that Mega Mouse is soft, nice and sweet.
She is very strong. Very, very strong.

And even very, very, very strong.

Everyone loves her. Children collect Mega Mouse posters. They have Mega Mouse binders, baseball caps, pens, and even Mega Mouse underpants!

Today the children are going on an outing with Mega Pig.

The bus takes off.
What a party: everyone sings and dances!

The wheels on the bus
go round and round,
round and round...

MEGA BRUSH
YOUR TEETH

Mega Pig starts a game of Eye Spy
with the children, when all of a
sudden...

BOOM!

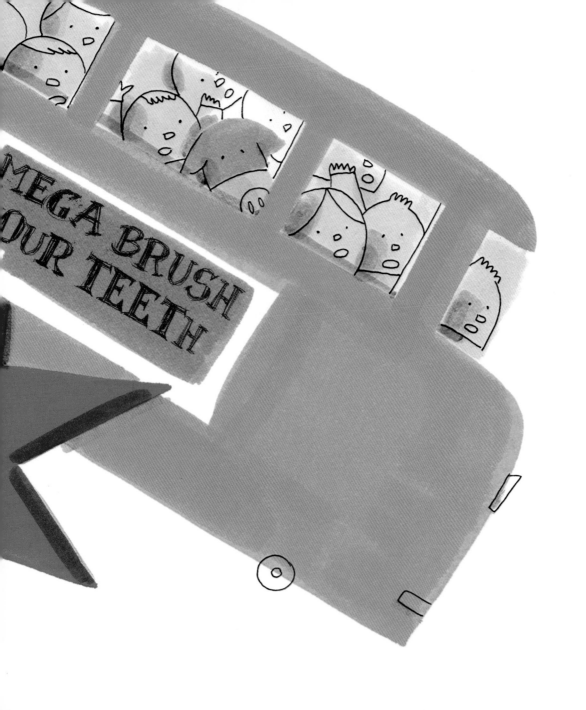

It's awful!

Another of the dreadful **Mosquito Man's**
dirty tricks!

He has destroyed the bridge, the bus is going to fall!

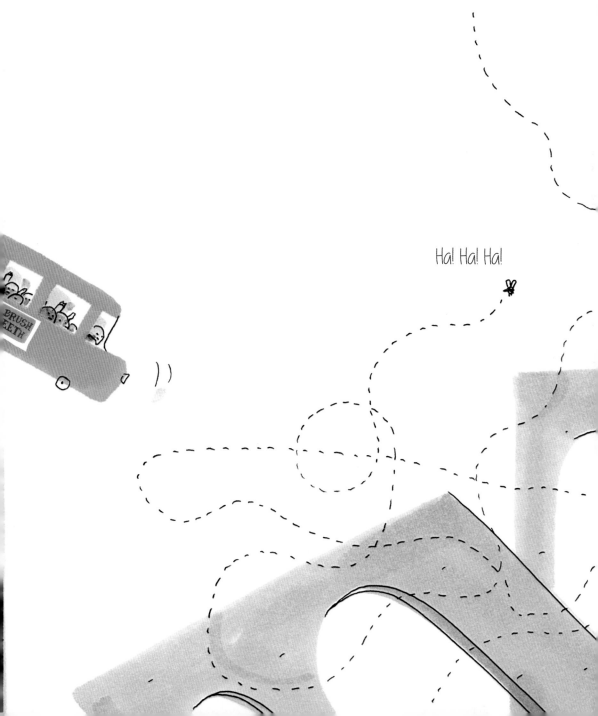

Mega Pig sends a message to Mega Mouse!

"Help!" cry the children.

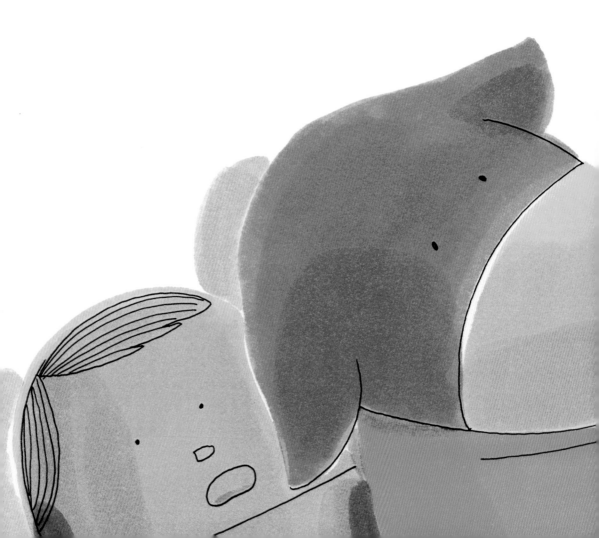

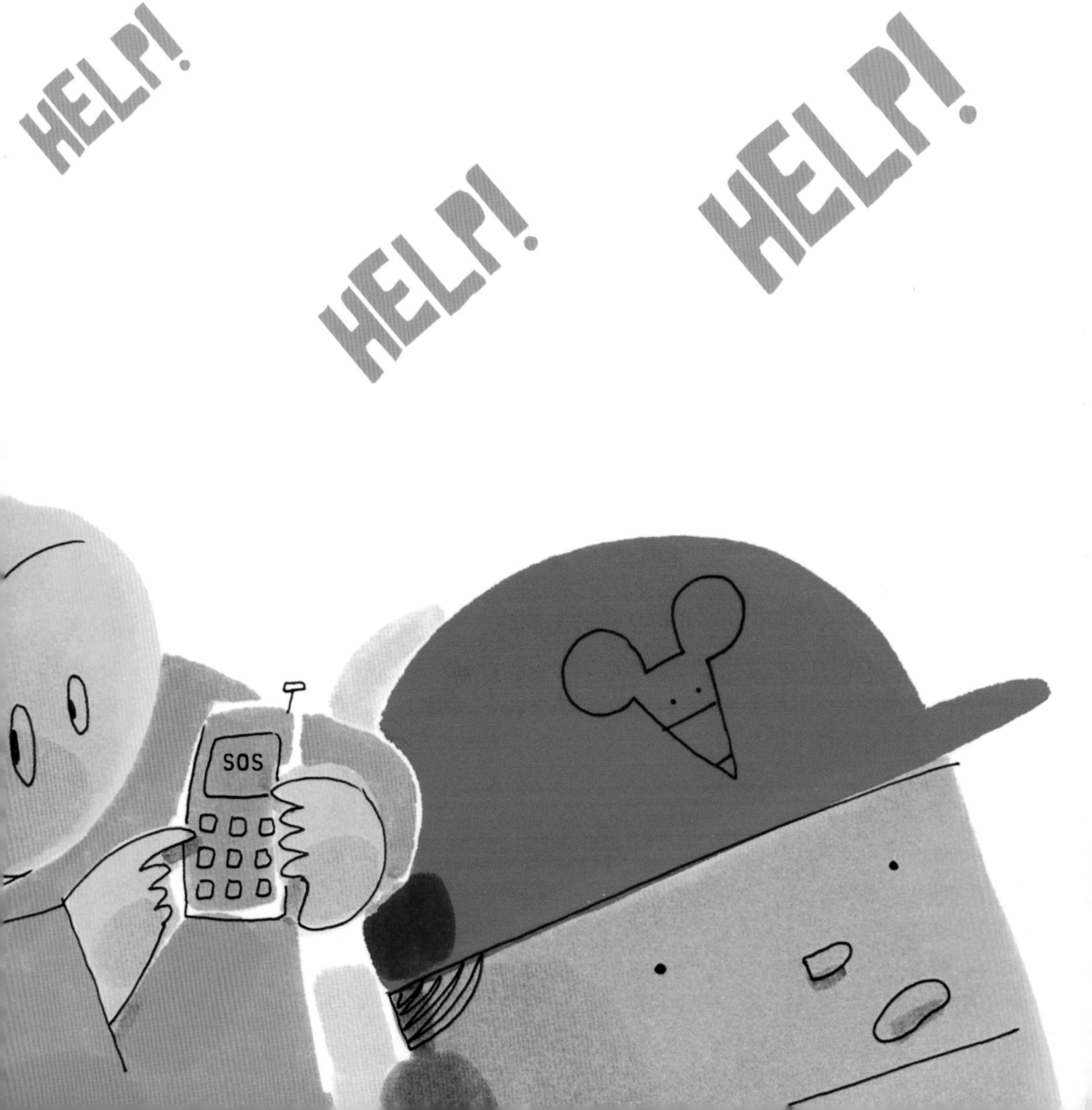
HELP!
HELP!
HELP!
SOS

Mega Mouse runs, she flies,
she is going to save Mega Pig and the children!
She is ready to fight if it's necessary.

I am ready to fight if it's necessary!

BUZZ! BUZZ!

It's too late, there is nothing you can do for them!

There's nothing Mega
Mouse can't do!

Look: she has stopped the bus from falling off the
bridge thanks to her super powers!

MEGA BRUSH YOUR TEETH

Mega Mouse has defeated the dreadful Mosquito Man (without using her disintegrating gun).

She lifted a bus without any help!

Mega Mouse is strong and courageous. She saved the children on the bus.

And...she is in love with Mega Pig.

Shhh...it's a secret!

MEGA BEAR

MOSQUITO MAN

MEGA PIG

MEGA CROC

MEGA PANDA

MEGA HIPPO